Dedication

"To every creative with a vision. Your world is beautiful."

Table of Table

NEW MOON

It was News Year's eve 2018, so the faculty and staff at the International Space Station South were celebrating yet another year of astrological discoveries. For the third consecutive year in a row their branch had been recognized as the top research group in the world. Dr. Tim Ross has a lot to do with that. As the International Space Stations South's top scientist, he has been at the forefront of all operations since filling the role, and lab progress has increased almost daily.

Tim Ross is a 25-year-old young black male, whom graduated from a number of prestigious universities and is considered by many to be a prodigy. He was born to two loving parents in his father Thomas, and his mother Donna.

They met in the urban middle-classed area of Queen City, North Carolina, where they eventually married and had Tim. Due to his natural intelligence and professional football player-like physique, he was a very confident man which enabled him to be very charismatic. That helped him to excel amongst his peers and gave him the drive to accomplish as much he could while still being at a particularly young age.

"Everybody on your feet!" says a man behind a podium placed on makeshift stage in the middle of the labs conference room. "Make some noise for the man who changed the balance of power in all of science, Tim Ross!" The room erupts into cheers as everyone in attendance applauds the man that has changed their lives.

Suddenly everyone turned their attention to a table located in the front of the room. Tim Ross then stands and begins to walk past the crowd of screaming adoration until he himself is the behind the podium. “Thank you, thank you, you’re too kind...” says Tim as the crowd starts to chant his name. “Ok, ok, I admit it. Yes, I am amazing, but do you know why? Because you’re all amazing!” he says as he points into the crowd. He goes on to give a speech that lasted about 20 minutes in total, thanking everyone for their contributions to the lab and ensuring them that their efforts do not go unnoticed.

Near the end of the speech Tim reveals that he has made a new discovery, one that may be his biggest yet. He informs everyone that over the last few nights he has been observing a strange new structure in space. With every passing hour, the object is becoming more visually clear in the ISS telescope.

"In all my years of studying science I never once even considered this a possibility, and it still feels funny saying this." Tim says as he looks in to the eager and intrigued faces of everyone in the crowd.

"I believe we have discovered a new moon orbiting the earth."

Puzzled looks swiftly plagued the faces of everyone in attendance before they began to throw a barrage of questions at Tim.

“What do you mean a new moon?”

“Is it new or has it just been hidden?”

“Does anyone else know about this?”

“How soon do you plan to explore?” asked the other scientist. The questions were coming so fast that it was hard for anyone to fully comprehend what was being said. There were very few pauses or moments for Tim to interject. Everyone’s word began to just run together, eventually resulting in an explosion of noisy chaos.

“Ok, settle down...” Tim says into the microphone having very little effect. That did very little to stop the ruckus. Majority of the scientist were still reacting as if they were kids giddy with excitement over an action movie. Loud and full of adrenaline.

Tim takes a step back from the microphone and waits for the initial reaction of his announcement to pass. About 45 seconds pass and the crowd noise begins to gradually decrease. Taking advantage of that opportunity, Tim walks back up to the microphone and begins to speak.

"Now that everybody has regained their sanity let's get back to business." He says joking as a portion of crowd laughed alone with him.

Tim then goes on to explain that he believes this moon is still in its infancy, and it would be a perfect opportunity to observe the growth of the organisms outside of the earth's atmosphere. If this new moon is inhabitable, then this will be the greatest scientific discovery of all time.

Humans could potentially normalize space exploration by establishing the first interstellar travel location.

"If people are willing to pay thousands of dollars to travel around the world, then imagine just how much they would be willing to pay to go to the moon!" Tim said with an emphatic tone, causing the excitement in the crowd to once again rise.

"Not only is ISS South the most accomplished scientific branch in the country, but we are about to be the richest in the world!"

Cheers once again start to pour out of the audience as they react like a high school basketball crowd after a game winning basket.

Tim tells them that rather than waste time celebrating the discovery, he plans to partake in an expedition to the new moon immediately.

"My entire life I've prided myself on being the best... working harder than everyone else, and being the first to do things. I see this task as being no different."

Tim goes on to tell them that he will be leaving the next day.

"The same resilience and work ethic we displayed to get to this point, are the same tools we'll use for this next breakthrough.

"So, prepare yourself," he says with a raised glass in his hand as if he were making a toast. "Tomorrow your life could change forever."

LOVE ISN'T SELFISH

"Babe I'm home," Tim yells up the stairs as he walks into the front door of his condo in the city. "Where are you?"

"We're in here," answered a faint voice coming from a bedroom.

Tim hurries up the stairs and enters a room where he finds his longtime girlfriend Vanessa.

Vanessa is a beautiful brown skin black woman, who stands about 5'5 with flowing shoulder length black hair and the shape of a professional cheerleader. The two of them met as freshman in college and had been dating exclusively ever since.

“How are you two doing?” he asked as he bends down and gently rubs Vanessa’s pregnant belly.”

“We’re doing fine,” she replied laughingly. “We just missed you, that’s all.”

“I missed you too,” Tim replied. “But I’m here now, and that’s all that matters,” he says as he softly kisses her on the forehead before taking off his suit to unwind after a long day.

After returning to the bedroom from a shower, Tim noticed that the vibe he was getting from Vanessa had changed. It was as if she had quickly become upset within just a few minutes.

He asked her what was wrong, she responded by asking him “so when were you going to tell me?”

Then, a deaf silence fell over the room for a few seconds until Tim finally reacted. He nervously asked what she was talking about while staring in the opposite direction to avoid making eye contact.

"One of your little scientist friends already posted about it on Facebook. You were really planning to leaving the planet tomorrow without so much as telling me," Vanessa says angrily while trying to hold back tears.

Pained and embarrassed Tim takes a few seconds to gather his thoughts before attempting to respond.

"Typical," Vanessa says while shaking her head.

"You're supposed to be one of the smartest people in the world, but you still can't figure out why you treat me as bad as you do...or why I let you."

"I... I was trying to figure out how to tell you. I really was. But I knew there was no words I could choose that would make you any less angry." Tim says.

"You're damn right I'm angry! We have our very first doctor's appointment as parents tomorrow and you're planning on skipping it to go play Buzz Lightyear."

Tim then took a few moments to gather his thoughts. He knew that he was in the wrong, but was too prideful to admit it.

"Please just hear me out," he said. "This could be the big break that we've been waiting for. Just imagine the possibilities of where this could go, the things we could buy , the places we could travel too..."

Vanessa was listening intently, but her face showed that her position on the issue was clearly unchanged.

Growing more frustrated by the second, she cuts Tim off and says, "the wedding you can continue to avoid" as tears burst from her eyes.

Tim quickly grabs Vanessa and hugs her as tight as he can. Still unable to think of comforting words, he begins to say, "I'm sorry" over and over again.

"You know you're going to be my wife, I just want everything to be perfect."

“That’s not it, and you know it” Vanessa says as she gently pulls away from Tim. “Since the moment I met you, one of the things that attracted me to you the most is your drive. Not only are you smart, but you always make sure that you get what you want. That’s not the issue though, the problem is that you’re selfish. Sometimes I feel like the only difference between you and a narcissist is that you don’t speak in the third person, but at the end of the day YOU always come first...”

Stunned and stricken with guilt Tim sits motionless at the foot of the bed. Realizing that every word Vanessa said to him had merit. He then swallows his pride and apologizes for his actions. Promising her that from that day forward he would no longer be avoiding responsibility.

After about 30 minutes of dialogue the two of them were able to settle their argument and once again embrace each other before the night was over.

"We still have one problem though," Tim says as he lays beside Vanessa. "I've already made the call to start the mission. I have guys prepping me for launch right now as we speak. I can't cancel."

"It's ok," Vanessa responds in an understanding tone. "You always were a go-getter, and when we met I promised I would never stop you. I would be contradicting myself if I got in your way. Can't call you selfish then turn around and be the same way, right?"

They looked in to each other's eyes and shared a good laugh, reassuring Tim that he could confidently take his mission the next day without any issues.

LIFT OFF

Tim wakes up earlier than usual and heads to the space station to get overnight updates on the new moon. Upon walking through the door of the observatory, he is greeted by one of the many scientists sitting behind the computers and telescopes. It was Dr. Alonzo Elliott, the same man that had introduced him at the ceremony the day before.

“I have something to tell you that I know you’re not going to believe,” says Dr. Elliott while smiling ear-to-ear and quickly approaching Tim.

“What is it?” Tim replies.

Dr. Elliott says, “While the launch team was doing calculations for your mission, they realized something odd, yet convenient for you I guess. This new moon is only 120,000 thousand miles away from earth..."

"...That's only about half the distance of our original moon, so you it will only take you a day and a half to arrive, rather than 3."

Tim looks at him in disbelief, "that's amazing!" he says while becoming growingly more eager to explore. "At least I don't have to be in the boring voids of space alone for days before I get there."

"You won't be alone, remember?" Dr. Elliott says before letting out a slight chuckle and pointing to a small room on the other side of the laboratory. "You have friends to water, and other friends to feed."

"Don't remind me," Tim replies. "I'm fine with watering the plants and all of the smaller organisms, but it's the animals that I hate dealing with. I'm not a zookeeper..."

"...I am an astronomer that happens to also be an astronaut. There are no puppies in space, at least not that I know of."

Dr. Elliott says, "Well isn't that the goal? To see if the species of the earth are able to inhabit the new moon successfully?"

Tim asserts, "Yeah that nice and all, but I think our focus should just be to see if humans can sustain life there. They are the ones that can pay us money. We can worry about building Seaworld later."

Tim spends much of his time after that conversation getting prepped for takeoff. Later that day it was time for commence and the mission to officially begin.

Before going to the shuttle Tim isolates himself for a few moments to call Vanessa to see how the doctor's appointment went. After receiving the news of good health for both she and the baby, he could now focus solely on the mission.

At approximately 1:00p.m that day Tim boarded a ship named Diggs 11 and broke through the atmosphere to begin his voyage to the new moon.

THE AURA

36 hours have passed and Tim has just successfully completed the landed sequence for Diggs 11. Before exiting the ship, he made sure to look around to see if there were any distinct differences between the new moon and the one that humans had reached before. He noticed that there was gravel floating miscellaneously through the air, large boulders were hanging in the air about 5 inches off the ground, and what seemed to potentially be a body of water in the near distance.

Eager and well-rested, Tim jumps into his space suit to prepare to depart from the ship. After making sure everything was functional and he had plenty of oxygen to last him, he took the very first steps ever taken onto the new moon. Leaving behind all the test subjects to first explore on his own.

The first thing that Tim noticed was the he could barely keep his feet on the ground while trying to navigate himself. On the original moon, the gravity is less dense, but things still have a measurable mass, whereas; on the new moon just about everything was completely weightless. So, he had to give up on traditional walking, and instead hopped and moved his arms in a swimming motions to propel himself in the direction he wanted to go.

"This is exhausting, it better be worth it," Tim thinks to himself as he was finally nearing the bizarre body of water he thought he had seen when he first landed.

As he got closer, he realized that this was no ordinary earthly water. It looked like a shiny blue liquid mineral that is foreign to the earth. The liquid wasn't flowing horizontally, but rather swirling and going upwards to what seem be no end, and crashing back down to the source to then repeat the process.

Tim speaks into a voice-note log built in to his space suit and says, "Note, a specific area of the moon seems to be weirdly effected by it's gravity. Blue liquid mineral resembling earth water is giving off radiant aura. Attempting to harvest for testing."

Then, he pulls a jar from a bag that's attached to the suit. He slowly approaches the space water cautiously, unknowing of just how wide the area being affected by the weird gravity is.

When he gets within arm's reach, he attempts to scoop some of the minerals into the jar. Then, when he tries to pull his arm back he is unable to.

"What the hell?" Tim blurts out loud as the pull of the current begins to overpower him.

He struggled mightily to get himself free, but with no gravity or proper footing he couldn't generate enough strength to pull away. So, within a few seconds his entire body was yanked in to the blue vortex. All alone, and unable to call contact anyone while away from his ship, he began to let out a terrified yell that could be heard throughout the cosmos.

Just as the panic was about was about to cause him to black-out, Tim began to think about Vanessa and the baby. About all the promises he had broken in the past, and how this was about to be the worst of them all. He had promised that he would return home safe and continue to provide for his family. Now, he was about to lose his life for the sake of riches and greed. Tears began to flow down his face as he prepares to meet his demise in anguish. Soon after, his consciousness faded to darkness as all he could see was the blue around him. Then, nothing...

After approximately 15 earth minutes, Tim begins to regain his consciousness. As he opens his eyes, the first thing that he sees is stars. Still dizzy from the apparent swirling, Tim noticed that he was now laying on the ground. He suspected that the vortex must have spit him out before killing him completely.

“Well I know not to try to touch anything else. I guess it wasn’t water after all if I’m still alive.” Tim says to himself as he prepares to stand.

As he plants his hand into the ground to posture himself, he notices that there is something strange going on with his arm. It feels heavier and it is glowing blue through the suit.

“Aaaaaaa...” Tim screams in fear as he begins to shake his arm to try to get whatever it is off to no effect.

“What is this? I know they didn’t add a new feature to the suit without telling me.”

He looks around and notices that he no longer sees the strange blue aura that had seemingly drowned him.

“You know what, I don’t even care.”

Then, he decides its time that he go back to the ship. Oddly, this time he is able to move a lot easier. He was no longer required to propel himself through the air, and he was able to walk normally without much resistance.

When Tim gets back onto the ship, he turns on the oxygen systems and heads to the sleep bunker to remove the suit. He finally gets to the upper body portion of the suit to remove the arm covering he had been curious about, and he is then greeted with an even bigger surprise.

The blue aura was coming from some kind of device that seems to have merged itself to Tim's wrist.

Displaying more fascination than fear, Tim's eyes grow wide as he immediately assesses it to be lost alien technology.

“This day just keep getting any weirder,” Tim thinks to himself as he attempts to pull the device of his arm with no luck. “Damnit, I can’t do anything here. I’ll have to handle this when I get back to earth. I’m not dead and I feel fine, so no reason for me to panic.”

After examining the device as much as he could, Tim decides it is time to contact the people at ISS South to let them know of all of the findings he had logged. Also, he told them to prepare for an emergency return. He will not be gone as long as originally planned due to a complication.

Most importantly, he let them know that he wanted to keep his return as secret until they are able to vet what findings they are willing to share...

...They are to keep everything confidential, even from the likes of the government. They could do nothing to stop them from threatening to cut funding or shut down operations if they wanted to.

With those orders commencing, Tim prepared the ship for emergency takeoff and created a list of tests and experiments he could conduct on the alien device while he spends the next 36 hours in space.

A THREAT AWAKENS

A day and a half has passed and the Diggs 11 is within 1 mile of the earth's atmosphere. Tim has finally reestablished a line of communication with the launch center and other scientist at ISS.

To prepare them for what they are about to see, he sends them all the audio notes that he had recorded during his time on the new moon, as well as the last 36 hours in space.

He was unable to deduce any information about the device that had attached itself to his arm, or find any effective ways of removing it.

"Hello... Hello, is anyone there? This is Dr. Tim Ross. Please prep the landing area for emergency landing!" he says in to the radio communicator frantically.

“Ross, what’s going on?” responded a voice coming from the communicator. It was Dr. Alonzo Elliott.

“We weren’t expecting you back for at least a few more days.”

“Zo... are you serious right now?” said Tim. “I request prep for an emergency landing and you start asking questions? I guess the messages I attempted to send before leaving the moon never actually made it to you all. Just get everything situated. We will speak more when I land.”

“My bad, you just caught me off guard. I was in the middle of my usual slacking off that I do around this time every day.” says Dr. Elliott. “I will have the launch team get everything ready immediately.

About 30 minutes later the Diggs 11 was once again initiating its landing sequence, but this time it was back on earth. Dr. Elliott and a large number of other ISS staff rushed out to the landing site to greet Tim. All of them ready to see the device that he spoke of in the audio logs they had heard over the last hour.

Tim could see them through one of the windows on the side of the ship, and it was obvious to him that he was about to be attacked with even more questions than he received at the New Years ceremony. Moreover, before he could bring himself to get off the ship, he couldn't help but think about how scared he was that his family would lose him when he was sucked into the vortex. Now, he could only think of her potential reactions if he had to walk in the house with a piece of unknown alien technology attached to his body.

"Well, no point in avoiding it." Tim thinks to himself before taking a deep breath and finally removing his seat belts to leave the cockpit.

As the door of the ship begins to open, natural light begins to fill the interior. The first thing he notices when his eyes focus is the supreme level of intrigue on the faces of everyone standing outside.

"It that it?"

"Is it causing you any pain?"

"Have you ever saw something like this before?"

"Have you figured out what it does?"

The crowd of scientists immediately began yell questions in Tim's direction as he slowly walks down the steps of the ship leading from the door.

“To answer all of everyone’s questions, I don’t know, I don’t know, please stop asking me I don’t know.” Tim responds in frustration as everyone stares at his covered yet still glowing forearm. “Let’s take this inside the lab. It’s supposed to be a secret remember?”

The team then reconvened in the testing wing of the ISS laboratory to begin tests and experimentation on the device. The process lasted about 16 hours and throughout the night, but the results were much to the dismay of the entire team. It was almost sunrise, and they did not have single new piece of learned information.

“I’m tired and this is starting to feel pointless,” Tim says as he struggles to stay awake while laying down and going through yet another test.

“After this one, I am definitely going home. I just want to see my wife and rest. I will deal with explaining it to her whenever it comes up.”

At the conclusion of the final test, the scientist conducting it once again informs Tim that he hasn’t found anything.

“Well, still nothing. That’s it for the night.” Dr. Elliott announces to the team. “Ross is going home, and he can’t leave his arm here, so that means we're all going home.”

“Thanks Zo.” Tim says as he gathers his things and prepares to exit the building. “I’ll call you when I wake up. No matter how tired I am, I doubt I’ll be able to sleep too well.”

Just as Tim was walking out the door, Dr. Elliott stopped him and jokingly said, "Hey Ross, sorry about all the questions earlier. I was mad you were interrupting my movie."

Tim looked at him with an amused smile on his face and replied, "That must've been some movie," and walked out of the building.

Just as he was about to reach his car, the device on his arm starts flash its blue glow, and the ground began to shake under his feet.

"Aaaaaa," Tim yells as he struggles to keep his balance before eventually falling to the ground.

"What as that?" he says, as he begins to stand up and brush himself off. "That couldn't have been an earthquake, not in North Carolina. That not common here at all."

A few moments later Dr. Elliott emerges from inside of the ISS building.

“Ross, you good?” he asks as he sees Tim still brushes dirt off his clothing.

“Yeah, I’m good. Did you feel that shaking too?” Tim replies.

“How could I not? Everybody in the building did. It’s a mess in there right now. Whatever that was did some serious damage. Do you think it was an earthquake?”

“That would be my first guess,” says Tim. “But something like that has never happened in my lifetime. Also, there and usually some kind of warning. Right?”

Dr. Elliott replies, “I study space just like you, don’t have me telling you lies.”

As the two of them continue you to talk, Dr. Elliott suddenly stops speaking mid-sentence, and a look of terror fell over his face. He points behind Tim and fearfully yells, "Woah! Who in the world is that?"

Tim turns around and is startled when he sees what appears to be a nearly 7-foot tall person dressed in a long black overcoat with a hood covering his entire body. He was standing about 50 yards away from them. Body motionless, as a slight breeze blows the tail of his coat.

Tim shouts, "What's your problem undertaker? You can just be sneaking up on people like that."

The strange person continued to stand motionless. Then, without saying anything he began to slowly walk in their direction. Suddenly, the device on Tim's arm begins to glow once again.

"Now here this thing goes again," says Tim while making sure not to take his eyes off the person for more than a few seconds. "This is private U.S government sanctioned property, you are not allowed to be here. Leave now, we have police on standby. They will be here within 5 minutes."

Just as Tim finishes speaking, the mysterious person stops walking and finally begins to speak.

"At last, after all these years of pain and suffering, my opportunity to get back at this filthy world has finally come..." he says in a deep raspy voice.

"Huh? Get back at this world? Please don't tell me you're one of those idiot that plans to steal a space ship or something stupid like that." says Tim unamused.

The mystery person then burst into an arrogant laughter. "Hahaha... space ship? Stupid slow-evolving bottom dweller, I don't need your primitive technology. I will have all that is necessary as soon as you hand over the Jericho!"

A large number of scientists began to poor out of the building as they saw what was going on through the interior windows.

"Dr. Ross, who is that guy?" asked one of them as he began to feel nervous seeing just how massive the mysterious person was up close. "If this is some kind of joke, then it is far from funny!"

"I don't think this guy is joking, but he is very confusing" says Tim. "He yelled out something about getting back at the world, and about something called the "Jericho"."

"Jericho? Never heard of it" replied the scientist.

"Look man..." says Tim to the still unidentified person as he begins to grow irritated.

"I don't know what you're talking about or what you want, but I'm not about to continue to go back-and-forth with someone who won't even show their face. Now take that stupid hood off you coward!"

The perplexing person once again let out laughter before starting to speak.

"A confident one I see, I guess the device may have actually chosen someone with some heart."

"How do you even know about this device?" says Tim. "We didn't report this to anyone, not even the government. There is no way that any information could've leaked that fast."

"I could sense it's energy as soon as you came through the atmosphere with it. It is unlike any other, I will always recognize it as long as my heart continues to beat."

Then, the mysterious person lifts his hand and begins to remove his hood, finally revealing his face.

Everyone, including Tim, let out an enormous gasp as they were shocked and sure to be haunted by what they saw in front of them. The mysterious person appeared to be a humanoid male, with two very distinctly horrifying differences. He had 2 horns growing top of his head and empty glowing blue eyes.

"Aaaaaaa," screamed many of the scientist as the quickly turned around and ran back inside the building. Leaving just Tim and Dr. Elliott outside with the creature.

"I am Lord, Warrior of The Skyy," says the creature.

“I have waited many millenniums for this opportunity. Watching as your non-apathetic species continues to destroy the planet you don’t deserve to inhabit in the first place. Now hand over the Jericho, and I will make this all happen a lot more peacefully.”

Visibly intimidated by what he was seeing take place, Tim says, “Millenniums? Who, I mean what are you? And this Jericho thing you keep talking about, it must be this thing on my wrist. Right?”

“Indeed,” Lord replied. “I have been here since very soon after the birth of the planet. In the beginning, there were 2 dominant races inhabiting the earth. The humans, which 70% of all intelligent beings were, and the remaining 30% was made up of The Skyy..."

"...At first, we all lived in harmony. Peacefully coexisting on the plains of Pangea. Then, after about 1,000 years, the population began to rises at alarming rate. The planet was still new itself, so it began to break apart the land mass as a form of self-cleansing. As a result, not only were the human and the Skyy civilizations broken apart, but also the natural resources they had access to were as well. The ruler of the Skyy civilization prophesied that one day the humans would realize the strength in their numbers, and let their greedy ways encouraged them to try to conquer us. Furthermore, although they had more people, our species was more evolved in terms of intelligence. We knew the attack would eventually come, so we had to arm ourselves with something that could even the odds..."

"...So, our greatest scientific mind, Artemis Jericho, discovered a water current along the coast that was odd. The water was flowing upwards. He concluded that this was one of the exactly locations that the earth uses it's force energy to push its land masses apart. Using early Skyy technology in tandem with many strong metals and minerals, Artemis was able to create a device that was could harness the push and pull force of natural gravity within the earth's atmosphere. With it, the user would be able to manipulate the gravity around them, using the energy it has stored. It could even be used to turn gravitational energy into physical energy that can be fired from the weapon. All the wearer must do is mentally push or pull in their mind, and aim..."

"...The only issue is, because it is essentially a creation from earth's energy, it is alive. So, it is a living thing and it chooses whomever it feels is worthy to use it."

Tim looks on in amazement before finally chiming in.

He says, "So your telling me that this thing on my arm has the power to do all of that? That's probably why I was able to move so easily when I was walking back to the ship on the moon. I had my mind on moving quickly, and that's exactly what I was able to do."

"Correct, gravity is no factor to he who holds the Jericho." Replied Lord.

"Ok," says Tim. "But that still doesn't explain why you're here, or how this thing got into space."

“When the war began, the humans quickly saw that even though they had more people in the war, the could not match the power of the Jericho. So, rather than continue to lose, they took extreme measures. They created a deadly disease filled plague and gave it to the warriors they felt were expendable. Then, they sent them on boats to conduct suicide missions on the shores on the Skyy civilization, leaving behind their disease-ridden corpses to spread germs. Because the plague was made up of germs that they hadn’t been exposed to in centuries, it killed off our almost our entire species within 5 years. In fear that the humans might try to steal the Jericho, Artemis took the weapon back to the location along the shore that he originally discovered the odd current..."

"...He threw it into the current where it became super charged and shot directly into the air, never to be seen again. I wasn't killed by the plague because I was an army warrior fighting and offshore battle at the time. When I returned, all that I knew and everything I loved was gone. Since then I've remained hidden in the shadows, waiting for the Jericho to return and an opportunity to avenge my people!"

LORD'S WRATH

The police arrive on the scene, and they quickly draw their weapons at the sight of Lord.

"Put your hands in the air and freeze!" yelled Captain Freddy Boyce, the current commissioner elect of the Queen City police department. "I have no idea what you are, but we've got a warm room in Area 51 waiting on you."

Tim says, "He tells me that he is from here, but I don't know how much of his story to believe. He clearly looks like an alien, but he was saying something about his people being extinct or something. Also, he was able to explain what this thing on my arm is. It doesn't seem like he has been lying."

“What thing on your arm?” responds Captain Boyce.

“Oh, uhhh...nothing,” says Tim, remembering that they hadn’t yet reported to anyone outside of ISS South about his findings on the new moon.

Lord’s face began to scrunch, showing that he was beginning to grow impatient.

"You naive humans think you know everything, but you are as you've always been. Insolent, smug, and audacious. You'd dare threaten me with captivity? IN THE NAME OF THE MIGHTY SKYY, I SHA'LL RID THE WORLD OF EVERY LAST ONE OF YOU EXPENDABLE INSECTS!"

He begins to run directly at the police.

"Ok men, FIRE!" yells Captain Boyce.

Every officer that had responded to the scene began to fire their weapons at Lord. There were eight squad cars in total, carrying about 20 officers. They unloaded hundreds of rounds in his direction causing a thick nontransparent cloud of smoke to form in front of them.

Captain Boyce yells out, "I bet he's not feeling so high and mighty now!"

About 10 seconds pass and a voice coming from within the smoke laughs and says, "I wouldn't be so sure about that."

As the smoke clears, the officers are in shock as they realized that their bullets had not harmed Lord at all.

"Hahahaha... after thousands of years you Neanderthals still haven't created weapons that can even scratch a Skyy warrior. Now it's my turn!"

Lord grabs a glove that had been hanging from his belt, and slides in onto his hand. Then, it begins to emit a blue aura.

"Woah, what is that?" Tim says to Dr. Elliott as they both stare astonishingly at the action from a distance. "That looks like that same blue aura that comes from this Jericho thing."

Dr. Elliott replies, "You're right, they are just about identical, but it doesn't look like the same device."

Just as he finishes speaking, Lord again starts to move towards the officers.

"I have grown tired of your interference! This will be the last time that you meddle in the matters of fate!"

Lord then leaps into the air before driving the glowing glove directly into the ground, causing a huge wave to flow through the pavement. The wave throws Captain Boyce and the other officers into the air about 15 feet.

"Aaaaaaa," they all screamed as their bodies flew uncontrollably through the air before crashing back down to the surface and badly injuring many of them.

Lord then turns his attention back to Tim.

"Now back to you," he says.

"Look you freak..." Tim replies. "...I don’t know what you just did, but you need to stop now!"

"Stupid boy, that was nothing. Did you think Artemis only created one weapon? Although the Jericho may be his greatest creation, he made personal weapons for the warriors of the war. This one just happens to be mine, and it's all I will need to defeat you."

Tim says "Listen here man, I’m not scared of anybody! This device has the potential to change me and my family’s lives, and I won’t let you or anyone else take that from us!"

"Very well then," says Lord. "Have it your way."

Then, he gathered himself before again leaping into the air, preparing to strike the ground to cause yet another shockwave. When he did, the Jericho started to glow.

Tim closes his eyes as he prepares for what is about to hit him. As the shockwave rolls through the ground under him, both he and Dr. Elliott are thrown off their feet into the air. When Dr. Elliott hit the ground, he landed on his back. That forced his head to whiplash, and caused him to lose consciousness.

As Tim's body was falling out of the air, it suddenly halted about a foot from the ground. Preventing him from sustaining any injury. When he finally opens his eyes, he's surprised to see himself floating in the air as if he were weightless.

"What's going on?" he says

"I guess that’s the Jericho's natural defense mechanism." says Lord. "Such a shame that such an amazing item can reside on the arm of a being so weak."

As Tim attempts to posture himself while still floating, Lord punches him in the back, forcing him into the ground with so much force that he creates a small crater.

Tim screams out in agony as it feels like his bones are being crushed under the pressure of a deep sea. With every connecting strike, Tim's screams become more and more faint, as his consciousness starts to slowly fade.

Lord says, "I have no mercy you! You are nothing more than a proxy of your people. Everything must always be about you. Disguising selfish intentions as good deeds for others, only to be their demise in the in the end. Well your karma has arrived, and The Skyy will rise again!"

Those were the last words Tim heard before blacking out and slipping out of consciousness.

Pressure Rises

"By the power invested in me, I now pronounce you, husband and wife."

"Congratulations you two, here is your beautiful baby boy."

"Native North Carolina astronaut discovers the first interstellar travel location."

While still unconscious, Tim falls into a dreamlike state, giving him visions of Vanessa and the life they were planning together. He wanted to prove to her that he had changed. He was finally ready to accept his own faults, and responsibility for his selfish ways. Now, he would yet again be proven to be a liar.

Soon after the pleasant visions stopped, the unnerving ones began. Hallucinations of Lord roaming the world and slowly killing off all of existence took over Tim's mind. He sees him using the Jericho to cause mass destruction. Breaking the foundations of mountains causing avalanches to fall on the towns below, causing floods in cities near ocean coasts, and forcing unsuspecting pilots to plummet to their deaths under the immense force of gravity. Then, the worst of them all. Tim sees Lord killing Vanessa with the assistance of the Jericho. The very device that he was responsible for bringing to the earth.

Enraged by the thought of losing everything he loves due to his actions, Tim feels his heart begin to race. The mental horror had finally ceased, and he starts to feel himself breathing again. While regaining consciousness, he feels an extremely heavy knee being driven into his back and constant tugging on his arm.

Not much time had passed. Lord had him pinned down while trying to remove the Jericho from his arm.

"Insolent human, you still breath?" he says. "I was going to spare your life and force you to watch the destruction of a world that you once loved, just I as I had to do. But I won't be able to do that because the Jericho seems to have chosen to permanently merge itself to you. Your death is the only way to ensure its removal. So, it shall be done."

Tears began to flow heavily from Tim's eyes as rage continued to fill his spirit. Not only was Lord planning treachery, but his arrogance showed that he would do it with no remorse.

While still in the crater Tim says, "You really think that you can kill the entire planet just because you lost a war a million years ago? You're sick! I don't care what your reason is. I refuse to let you harm my family or any other person on earth. If you're here because of me, then I'm going to make sure you're gone because of me!"

As Tim's adrenaline flowed the Jericho began to glow and he could feel a tremendous flow of energy course through his body.

Suddenly, he clinched his fist while pulling away from Lord and roared at the top of his lungs, "GET OFF ME!" Then, the Jericho fired off a powerful energy blast knocking Lord back about 30 feet through the air.

"Woah!" Tim says in complete shock as he is finally able to stand up. "I feel amazing, like my body just reinforced itself. It must be the energy from this thing. I guess that's what he meant when he said it can be used as a weapon. Well so be it, Artemis whoever, you'll get your wish."

As Tim walks out of the crater, he sees Lord slowly standing up. He is grabbing his shoulder which seemed to have absorb much of the blast.

"Such power does not belong in the hands of the inferior!" says Lord. "How dare you harm a warrior of The Skyy! For that, you will parish as this world burns!"

Lord pulls another glove from his belt, similar to the one he was already using.

"Now, we fight to the death. Shall I die in combat, I will die with honor. I would have it no other way.

Lord then claps his hands together in Tim's direction causing a power boom of force energy. That energy threw Tim backwards, forcing him through the large glass windows of the ISS building.

The scientist inside the building begin to visibly panic. They ran through and from the building attempting to find somewhere to hide, screaming at the terror of what they were witnessing.

"Well I didn't see that coming," Tim thinks to himself as he lies on the glass ridden floor.

He then stands up. His clothing is badly tattered and he is deeply wounded on many parts of his body.

Tim walks back outside to see Lord once again laughing arrogantly.

"Hahaha...you barely know how to use that thing. You really think you stand a chance?" says Lord.

"It has nothing to do with chance. I'm Tim Ross, I've never been a loser and I won't start today. It's time to finish this, let's do it."

Tim's feet begin to hover over the ground as the Jericho glows, and he dashes through the air to through a punch at Lord.

Lord blocks it, then retaliates with punches of his own.

The exchange lasted for about 2 minutes before Tim was able to land a flush punch to Lord's chin, knocking him forcefully to the ground.

"Give up you piece of trash! I'm ready for this weird ass day to be over." Says Tim.

Lord replies, "Surrender is only an option for the weak. It's an easy concept for you fathom because the blood of the unworthy surges through your veins."

In an attempt to catch Tim off guard, Lord slammed both of his power gloves against the ground while still he was pretending to be hurt on a bended knee. That caused a shockwave twice the size of the one before.

As the ground broke in to pieces and shot upward under him, Tim used the power of the Jericho to balance on 2 pieces of broken asphalt, and suspend himself in the air where he was out the reach of harm.

"Try again. I think I'm getting the hang of this thing." Says Tim. "Now it's time to finish this.

Tim uses the push force of the Jericho to throw one of the police squad cars at Lord. As he dodges it, he takes his attention away from Tim for just a second. When he turns around, he is gone.

“Where did you go?” Lord yells as he looks around confused.

“RIGHT HERE!” Tim yells from behind Lord as he raises the Jericho to his lower back. “If shooting this thing into space kept it off the planet for all this time, then let’s try the same with you!”

“What?”

“TAKE THIS!” screams Tim as he fires an energy blast into Lord, propelling him directly into the sky.

The blast was so powerful that it was able to push Lord’s body through all the restrictions of the atmospheric pressure. He now resides in the recesses of space.

The Queen City Hero

Two weeks have passed. Terry Jordan, Mayor of Queen City is holding a town hall celebration downtown for Tim to celebrate the courage and heroism he displayed while defending their fine town.

"Hello and welcome, to all of the fine North Carolinians that came out today to celebrate with us on this joyous occasion. I, Terry Jordan, Mayor of Queen City, would like to officially declared the 23rd day of May each year from here out to be "Tim Ross Day." Just 2 weeks ago our great city was in danger of being destroyed by an extraterrestrial being that can only be identified as Lord. He caused massive earthquakes which resulted in many buildings collapsing, our sewer system being blocked by cratered asphalt, and in total an estimated 20 million dollars' worth of damage..."

"...All in less than 2 hours, and with basically just his hands. According to those that were at the scene when it took place, he even spoke about ending the entire human race. Luckily, this world has no room for that type of villainous behavior. So, when all was in doubt, good once again triumphed over evil, and our hero emerged. I want everyone to stand on their feet, and put your hands together for the man himself, Tim Ross!"

The crowd of over 100,000 people began to clap and shout praises at the top of their lungs. People were lined up for miles for the chance to see a potential real-life superhero.

Before approaches the microphone to address the crowd, Tim turns to Vanessa and gives her a kiss. The two of them share and intimate stare before he turned away to walk. More than any of the notoriety he was about to receive, Tim was glad to be with the love of his life again. He was no longer worried about disappointing her.

Tim stands in front of the microphone for nearly a full minute before speaking, just to embrace the continuing cheers.

“What’s up Queen City? I hope everyone is enjoying themselves. First of all, thank you for the support. This event would not have been possible if it weren’t for you..."

"...Like Mayor Jordan said, I am Tim Ross. Just under a month ago I went on a space expedition to a mysterious new moon that our ISS South telescopes revealed to our scientist. Upon carrying out that mission I came in contact with a strange ancient device only identified as the Jericho. With it, my natural physical strength and skills have all be extremely heightened. Also, it allows me to manipulate the push and pull forces of gravity. At this current time, I am unable to deduce any further information about the device, but our team of scientist will continue to work around the clock until we have more answers. Furthermore, I want to take this moment to instill confidence in the public that I have no ill intentions or heinous plans for the future..."

"...I am here to continue to assist with astrological discovery, and to protect the city if a situation becomes dire. From now on always remember, THE QC HAS ME!"

The crowd then explodes with cheers as Tim raises both hands in the air like a heavyweight champion. He was solidified and complete embraced.

As the celebration was nearing its close, Mayor Jordan return to the microphone to address Tim one last time.

"Ok Tim, everyone wants to know. The elephant in the room is, everybody knows that every good superhero has an alias. What should we call you?"

Tim grabs the microphone and looks into the crowd with a mischievous grin on his face and says, "You can call me Pressure."

www.ingramcontent.com/pod-product-compliance
Ingram Content Group UK Ltd.
Pitfield, Milton Keynes, MK11 3LW, UK
UKHW051136260726
13967UKWH00010B/3085